PodWarp

Gil Hardwick

Published by Crusader eBooks, Perth, Western Australia

Copyright © Gil Hardwick 2006-2010

Cover image: *http://boles.com/called/06/eug1.jpg, June 2006*

Cover Design by Gil Hardwick

The right of Gilbert John Hardwick to be identified as author of this work has been asserted by him in accordance with the provisions of the Australian Copyright Act 1968.

National Library of Australia Cataloguing-in-Publication entry:

Author: Hardwick, Gil.

Title: Podwarp / Gil Hardwick.

ISBN: 978-0-9872987-5-1 (paperback)

Dewey Number: A823.4

CONTENTS

Book I

This last warp had been nasty, leaving Babineau nauseous and unfocused. The livestock containers had come through intact, and the grain and vegetable bins, but even the routine unloading of them had been a unusual chore. The solar flares, he thought.

As they finished he let the transport drivers go early while his gauchos herded the last lots of cattle into the pens overnight, ready for the slaughterers and processors to start work early next morning.

That done he stripped of his working gear and took the elevator up through the air-locks from the vast industrial understory complex below into the showers and purifying vents, and thus cleansed of possible contaminants up again into the towering quarters of the pod proper far above.

He stepped out into his own apartment, but instead of dressing went straight through to his sleeping bay and slipped quietly under the covers, leaving the flag up not to be disturbed while he settled.

Eventually a light knock at the door drew him awake and he pulled on a gown to answer it, to find his housekeeper there with a draft for him, and signing, "Monsieur Babineau", that a light meal had been prepared.

His disorientation aside, the same culture-shock he always felt on returning left him walking past the servant without acknowledgment.

The shimmering field enclosing the pod, making the sky a sickly pink apparition compared to that over the outstations where their food was grown, only partly disturbed him. He had learned to ignore it. After all, it only kept the weather out, and the humidity and temperature within at steady comfort, costing them naught on good days but the soft fluffy white and clear blue.

It was the podlings themselves, ostensibly servants as they themselves happily admit, all plugged in and connected together via their micro-chip implant constantly receiving instructions, and off-duty their unending podcasts, streaming videos and music, news, blogs and chats, and subscription e-lectures in society and philosophy, psychology and the state of the environment, as prelude to advancement, that left him ill at ease.

They must think it wonderful, he surmised, he among their nominated lords and masters to feed them, or so they deferred, and keep them safe, with them content to serve meals and tend the long streets and corridors and apartments, cleaning the carpets and toilets, their complexion so fair, unblemished.

One might be happy for them, except while their eyes saw everything they looked at nothing, their thoughts so taken up with receiving and sending messages, and keeping in close touch with friends and loved-ones far and wide, and life-long learning and education; and music, always music, silent as not to disturb anyone but internally dark metal, or rocking, or symphonic, or popular or country. You could see the bandwidth in their walk.

It was their connectedness that bothered him, but he ate his meal in silence while his thoughts wandered off toward the new ranch ready for harvest during the next warp.

The gauchos would have left already, not bothering to come up through the pod sterilisation process merely to wander about the endless corridors, and whore and drink themselves silly, wasting their pay; simply gone again while they had the chance once the warp gate coordinates had been recalculated, before the clock was reset to the new cycle sealing the pod from the outside.

At least they were safe. They were always safe, apart from the warp itself; the folding in time/space that let them travel, always avoiding droughts, and plagues, and wars; always planting and harvesting during the best seasons wherever and whenever they found them.

His own job was less safe, but manageable and well paid for that, and it gave him status, not merely as commodities broker but for his diplomacy and friendliness, and his equipment and crew always in good order, and with that good standing among the peoples whose land they periodically claimed for their crops and herds; allowing him his tattoos of rank and leaving them plenty in compensation.

It may not always be that way, he knew, depending on the pod's demands, and how happy the podlings, but things worked out for now.

The draft had relaxed him, and finishing his meal he went and showered again, this time in the clear fragrant waters distilled by the podshield itself, which produced it as rain collected on pristine roofs and gutters, in the upper storey, and draining down into the cisterns. He stepped into the drying chamber, then out into his master bedroom where his town clothes were laid out for him.

He dressed and went out. There was a live show at his club, and he had a choice of that or a game of bridge if there were a tournament in progress.

But as he made his way through the crowd he began to sense eyes looking at him, which was odd because none of the other Kadians lived hereabouts, and podlings never looked at anything.

Continuing along the corridor he slowed and turned into an elevator lobby to stand waiting for a lift up to his club. The odd feeling stayed with him. He looked down to see a snowy head of hair right next to his elbow, and as the lift arrived and he moved to enter it came with him.

"OK." He said, to nothing in particular, then as he came to his stop and the doors slid open he stepped out and went over to a settee in the lobby and sat down. It sat next to him.

"Supposing I were to be wondering what a podling boy would be doing following me around, and sitting next to me, how would that be," he mused aloud.

The boy snapped up at him, startled by the question, but he had no answer to give, or was shy; embarrassingly so. His unblemished skin glowed bright pink, as his eyes stared bright liquid right into his face.

"Scared, eh? No problem," he said, then stood and re-entered the lift. Inside, with the noise of the motors backing him, he squatted to bring his face level with the boy's. Turning him around to face the wall away from him, he reached up and parted his hair right where the implant would have been injected at birth. Nothing amiss, the tiny lights flickering there as expected through his pale scalp, he turned him to face him again.

"Your name?" he asked.

"solxv98fg6", the boy snapped to attention.

"Ha!" Babineau. "Don't fuck with me. What is your name?"

"Sola."

"OK. What happened to your implant?"

The boy looked away, then back, and away again. "Nothing happened to it. It's just boring."

"There was no malfunction that you could detect?"

Sola looked at him curiously, then snuggled in close, eye to eye. "No, it works alright. But I figured it out. You won't tell anyone?"

"Who would I tell? I am my own man already. What do you want to say to me?"

The boy smiled, relaxed, then leaned in close to his ear.

"Any time you think louder, the volume goes down. The boring stuff they put in you. I mean. So that leaves you to think."

Babineau pushed the boy back off his lap, still watching his face, and his not unhappy smile at the discovery.

"Why are you telling me this?" he asked. "Why me?"

Disappointment showed abrupt. Intense.

"OK. I am Kadian, alright," he said, then walked away back into the lift down to his residential level. Forget the club.

The snowy-head shadow didn't leave him. He knew that once the implant had been made they were orphaned and individuated, made dependent on the implant sitting there in the back of their brain for knowing, and him and his like for sustenance. It was one way or the other, connected or not as the case may be, but for now a decision had to be made.

If this kid was able to think; smart enough to figure out how to adjust his implant at will, and interact with what was happening around him, it meant he was capable of synthesising ideas. That could either make him useful, or dangerous.

"Sola", he looked down, wanting his attention. "Where do you stay?"

They walked on while the boy thought before answering. "I can't get in. My login was canceled." Then, pausing, he looked up. "I was thinking about getting some bits together for a new control circuit . . . you know . . . for a remote camera I could poke through the shield, so I could see the sky . . . the real blue sky . . . and I forgot, and missed verification. So the pod thought I malfunctioned and was processed."

"Processed? No. What brought you to me?"

The boy stopped, astonished, and he turned to meet his gaze.

"Coz you're the man, Henri Babineau. Everybody knows you."

"What? No. I am nobody. Nobody knows me. I come and go, bring the food in and go out again. I calculate the next warp, I play cards at the club, or watch a show, then I go out again, that's it."

He looked down, as if to say why am I telling you this, but what he got back was adoration. The all too accustomed podling seeing but never looking flashed through his mind, except this one had taken the extra step.

"You are famous." The boy said. "We are always receiving downloads of your adventures. Every kid knows you."

He looked down sharply. Good God, he thought. They never look at me, only their image of me, inside their heads. Now this kid thinks that is the real me, and here I am. Fucking cartoon character come to life. He didn't wake up, I came to life.

"What am I going to do with you?" he asked out loud.

The kid shrugged, grinning happily.

Back at his apartment he punched in his PIN and waited for the iris scan, and the door hissed softly open.

"Maigret!" he strode in calling out loud, his heels barely heard on the soft thick carpet. No answer.

"He went out," the boy said. "Nobody thought you would be home yet."

He stiffened, and thought a moment, then looked down.

"OK," he said. "OK, what next?"

He paused a moment, then added, "I tell you what. You sit over there, and I sit here, and you explain to me this endlessly interesting conversation you have with yourself."

The way Sola went and sat down impressed him, head down and a little sheepish while he thought. Naïve, but brave, and honest for that.

"Well," he said finally. "I don't know what to do. I don't get any lessons or instructions anymore. My instructions, I mean, telling me what to do next. When I forgot to stand by for verification I was logged out. The motor circuits took me a while to figure out, and I forgot to stand by, then the page timed out and I couldn't get back online. But I still get all the news, and everything else, so I can listen to what is going on. That's all."

Babineau studied him, curiously. "So, how did you know Maigret would be out, and when I was supposed to be home?"

"We know your habits. You are so famous; everyone knows when you go out to the club, and how long you stay. The cameras are there."

"Are they now? Why would they want to be watching me?"

It was the boy's turn to study him now. He stared at him a moment, bewildered. "Don't you know?"

"Know what? What am I supposed to know?"

"The Happiness Purpose. You are our hero. Every time we see you are back home it is a celebration."

"What? Celebration? Inside your head?"

"Yes, of course. Victory celebration. It means we are winning the war, and that makes everyone happy."

"War? What war? We are farmers. We grow the food."

"No. You are the warrior against evil . . . the forces of evil . . . the war never stops, that is why you have to go out all the time."

He shook his head. "This is madness," he muttered, shaking his head, then looked up again.

"So who are these forces of evil?"

"We don't know. They can strike from anywhere, suddenly and without warning. That's what makes them so evil. So every time you return it means you have survived and triumphed."

"OK!" he stood suddenly, "enough of this. Come with me."

Maigret had returned and was standing patiently in the corridor, and Babineau quickly rattled off his instructions for a new warp. The calculations had already been made, and the coordinates set to allow the gauchos onto the next ranch, to work the season until he arrived to grade the produce and negotiate prices. So, a quick trip in and out to show the boy what he actually did only meant breaking the seal briefly.

He turned back inside, placing his hand on the boy's head, steering him toward his elevator down into the understory. Back in the apartment, he stopped and began to disrobe, ordering the boy to strip and leave his sterile pod clothing behind.

He stripped naked while the boy stood, staring at him. Then the t-shirt and sneakers and baggy shorts went, but he stopped there, reddening with embarrassment in his pale skin and lime-green satin boxers.

"Come on," he said, "right down. You cannot pass through the air locks like that."

The boy had an erection, he could see. Thinking for a moment, he turned him into the shower and ran the cold tap full blast for half a minute of so, then leaned down and helped him drop the now soggy boxers and stepped him into the dryer. Dry but distracted now, and still shivering, Sola simply followed him obediently into the elevator.

Down, down, down through the air locks, they came out onto the loading ramp before the warp gate. He steered the boy with his hand on his head again, into the change room and sat him down while he dressed in his newly cleaned outside clothes, then went to find something for him to wear. Some of the gauchos were short, and their sons and nephews came with them occasionally, learning the business, and there were always changes of clothing for them. Eventually he found something about the right size, that would do the job at any rate.

Dressed up in a cowboy outfit restored his spirits, and Sola went to look at himself in a grimy old mirror screwed to the wall. Babineau plonked a hat on his head, and that done bade him follow.

The warp gate was softly humming now, since the seal had been breached, so they simply walked straight through. Only a slight blurring of vision accompanied their passing, and they came out onto a fairly broad track leading into a village or town of sorts. Two men on horseback were waiting for them, leading another saddled horse which Babineau mounted, then reached down and pulled the boy up behind him.

They turned and rode on into the village, past the outlying houses as people stopped to wave, and boys ran out after them yelling and laughing, until they came to a larger building that seemed like a long hall. There they dismounted, as a group of old men and women came out to greet them. A crowd gathered.

Then an old lady came to the fore, hobbling, and supporting herself with a stick. Everyone went quiet while she looked the boy up and down, then stepped up to him and removed his hat. She ran her bony fingers over his scalp, then examined his ears, and eyes and nose, and finally inside his mouth, poking a finger down his throat. Then she unbuttoned his shirt, and felt his skin and ribs, up and down.

She turned to Babineau, gazing at him keenly, knowing.

"Henri, sometimes you are stupid." she said. "You bring him out? This pod boy. You know they cannot survive outside. He will sicken and die here, you know that."

"Oh, I don't think so. Maybe he will be sick," he conceded. "But he won't die. He woke up and turned down the implant, and started to think, that is all. He is very bright; very sharp, and clever. He will resist. But right now his mind is full of shit."

"Ah!" she said, then turned Sola's head toward her. She gazed deeply into his eyes, then nodded, and taking his hand turned to lead him inside. The boy resisted, holding back, looking at him in askance. The old lady demurred, and he nodded. Turning to the assembled town he bowed his apology and followed them inside.

"Sola," he said. "This old lady is the matriarch and healer. You must forget your war games. Out here your skin is too soft, and your gut. You will get sunburn, or cancer, or infection, and if you do you will die. So you must be inoculated, OK?"

"How old is he?" she asked, still dragging him along by the hand.

"How old are you?"

"Eleven."

"No. You are not eleven, only Year Eight. Your classmates are eleven, not you. You are too bright for that. Maybe the grading scale recalculated your age because of your outcomes advancement, or maybe you just think you are older. If you were eleven you would be in Year Ten already. I say you are eight, just turning nine."

The boy looked miserable.

"Sola," he went on. "Trust me. If you were eleven you could die out here. Puberty is too close. If you are eight your body will have a chance to adjust first, before the changes start."

By then they had turned off the main hall into a side room, and the crone stopped abruptly and bade him undress.

"She has a poultice," Babineau explained. "It will thicken and toughen your skin, and protect you from the sun. There is no shield out here, you see, that is all."

This time the boy nodded, and undressed himself. He let her work the dark foul-smelling mud up and down his body, in and out, every nook and cranny. When she finished she turned him around to face her, then with a bony old finger dug a wad out of her mouth she had been chewing, and opening his own mouth pressed it in between his teeth, over his tongue.

"Chew it," Babineau said, "then swallow. Swallow a few times if need be, and we will give you some soup. It has all the gut flora, for your tummy, and your bowel, so you can digest the natural food we have out here, OK?"

He did so, almost gorging on the sickly-sour taste not just filling his mouth but running down his throat, into his stomach, then as she took him up again for a bath Babineau held them both pause.

"Sola. After we go outside again, after your bath, you should call this lady great-grandmother. I call her mother, so you call me grandfather. Then things will be well for you." He stood and went out.

Into the warm bath the old lady threw bundles of herbs, squeezing and crushing them to extract the liquid, the poultice quickly reacting to it, and soon he could feel his whole body tingle. She washed and massaged him all over, rubbing the goo into his skin, then that done stood him up and hosed him down with clean water.

One blessing was that she allowed him to dry himself with the towel she proffered, but that was short-lived as she took hold of him again and, oiling her hands from a flask, rubbed him all over again leaving a slick film over his entire body.

"Now, child," she said, "You can get dressed. I give you this oil. You must massage it all over, twice a day, until it is all finished."

He took it, and turned to dress, but she held him.

"Yes, grandmother," she said. "Yes, thank you *abuela*. Thank you, *noña*."

He looked at her strangely, but she prompted him, chucking his chin as she would a toddler, gazing directly into his eyes, insisting, and holding him to it.

"Thank you, grandmother," he said, shyly.

"And you will not forget the oil. Twice every day, when you rise in the morning and after your bath in the evening, before you go to bed - until it is all finished."

"I will not forget, grandmother. Thank you for looking after me." He was learning.

"Good boy," she said. Now you can dress, and go join your grandfather Henri.

She stood, and taking up her stick she tottered out, sighing and mumbling to herself. Sola dressed quickly, then made his way back out into the main hall where Babineau was sitting talking quietly with the old men. As he came up, they stopped and turned to acknowledge him.

He went and stood next to Babineau. "Now I stink," he complained. "This stuff is terrible. And I've got a tummy ache."

The other chuckled. "Yes, you came here on an empty stomach. Sorry about that, but it will save your life."

He pulled up a chair and bade him sit, then ladled a great bowl of soup from a big crock on the table. "Here, drink this, it will make you feel better. And eat some bread too, and cheese we have here, and some meat. Eat your fill." he continued. "When you finish there is some fresh fruit for you, as much as you want."

The boy tried the soup, tentatively, just a sip in the spoon, but it was delicious and soon he finished the entire bowl before reaching for bread and cheese. One of the old men next to him took the soup bowl, and set a plate down in its place. He had not realised he was so hungry, and they all looked on happily as he devoured the meal.

"So," Babineau said finally, "You will survive. Now I have some bad news I am afraid."

He looked up, sharply, staring him in the eye, but the other just smiled as he caught the twinkle. "These people here are your forces of evil, my boy. Look at them."

He looked around, then giggled, embarrassed. "No they are not!" he exclaimed. "The forces are big and fat and ugly. They are hairy, and have long claws, and glaring red eyes, and stink real bad. Besides, they believe different things from us, and wear turbans and long robes, and eat children, and beat their wives."

They all looked at each other, then back at him, faces blank with astonishment.

"Sola." Babineau leaned over, taking his attention. "Can you still hear the news?"

He sat for a moment, his eyes losing focus as he listened. "I can only hear bits. There is a lot of static."

"If we went close to the gate, could you hear then?"

"Maybe," he shrugged.

Babineau stood and waved his hand, and they all rose to follow him outside. There they made a progression along the road, passing through the outlying buildings toward the gate. As it came in sight Sola stopped, listening.

"I can hear now." he said.

They all stopped, as he stepped slowly closer to the gate until he was happy with the signal. He looked up at Babineau, then listened again, eyes widening.

"There you are," he said, triumphant. "It is true. There was a new uprising, and you had to leave suddenly. The fighting has intensified, and there are grave fears for your safety."

They all looked at each other again.

Babineau knelt down and shook him back into focus. He looked at him, astonished.

"Sola, this is me here. Am I fighting?" he cried, as loudly as he could without frightening him too much. "Do you see forces arrayed against me? I came out with you, did I not?"

The boy went pale, white as a sheet, then collapsed in his arms. He was still breathing, so he picked him up and passed him over to one of the younger men with instructions to take him back to the hall and let him rest. Then he turned on his heel and strode back through the gate.

Inside on the loading bay he went straight across to the change room, where he stripped and entered the elevator up again through the showers and air locks.

Back in his apartment, he dressed, then called for Maigret. No answer came, so he went out into his living room where a new face appeared.

"Where is Maigret?" he wanted to know.

"Ah, Monsieur Babineau, I am Philippe. Your former servant suffered a happiness breakdown, poor man. He has been processed. Please come this way, some gentlemen from the Ministry are waiting to speak with you."

Book II

When they had finished their day's work the boys were allowed to sit near the warp gate so Sola could listen to the news, and watch movies. If there was only news he would relate it to them as he listened, but once he became engrossed it was boring for them and inevitably they wandered off to play, or simply went home.

The podling boy brought out by Henri Babineau had adapted to living outside well enough, his great-grandmother Juanita making sure he ate plenty of wholesome food, making sure his plate was piled high, and that he ate it all, and applying her poultice to his skin whenever the boys went swimming, or he forgot to wear his hat, and long sleeved shirt and trousers, and he came in burned.

For some time he had suffered periodic bouts of diarrhea that had left him spent and exhausted, but that settled eventually and with the hard work he started to put on weight, and add solid muscle to his slender frame.

Babineau came and went, never the same it seemed; a sadness on him that had not been there before, especially when he happened to glance his way. But apart from that he was good to him, always enquiring after his health, and his progress. The family who had taken him in were all related through Juanita, so it was one big extended family with plenty of aunties and uncles, and brothers and sisters and cousins.

The men went away a lot, working for Babineau. From inside the Pod he could calculate which gate they would exit on each warp, so they traveled widely, all over the world, but always returned to the right time so it seemed as if they had been gone only a day or so, when in their own lives a whole year had passed, or better. So the boys had less free time than they wanted, and sometimes the older boys went and they missed them, but life was good and they did not complain.

Except that sometimes Sola missed the Pod terribly. It had been the whole of his life, until he stopped listening and started experimenting and mucking around, and made a mistake.

Except that his hero turned out to be not quite the hero he thought he would be, and here he was, out here, farming wheat and sheep, and feeding pigs, and running cattle instead of fighting wars, in his mind anyway, and facing sadness instead of being happy and returning triumphant to accolades and rejoicing.

Being happy is good. Of course it is a good. Being happy is, well, being a hero, to a lot of people. Being sad is bad, because it made people depressed. How could anyone be so inconsiderate, so cruel? Why didn't things work out?

One day, as he sat near the gate apparently in a deep trance, one of his aunties came up and blew in his ear, then when he did not move she slapped his head, then reached down and took his hand, and lifting him up off his stool dragged him back home.

On the way past the village hall great-grandmother Juanita called to her from the doorway, "Rosa, don't be so rough on the boy."

Auntie Rosa turned on her. "He is useless!" she cried in frustration.

The old lady gazed at her a moment, then beckoned. "Bring him here," she said patiently. "Henri will be back this evening. He can talk to him."

Sola hesitated, then asked if he could wait for Babineau back at the gate, and anyway he had not finished the assignment he had been working on since being interrupted by Auntie Rosa.

They both stared at him, then shrugged, resigned to his ways, and turned and went back to their respective chores. He stood there a moment gazing after them, then turned back the way they had come, inclining his head slightly as he walked trying to pick up the signal again.

Distracted, and not expecting anyone until later, Sola failed to notice the gate shimmer and Babineau with his gauchos emerge. But for the fact that he was still a distance away he would have wandered into them, but they saw him there and pulled up to wait. As he drew near Babineau dismounted and handed the reins to one of the men, then knelt to greet him; and when he failed to respond took him by the shoulders and looked him in the eye before holding him gently in his arms. Without ado, he swung the boy onto his back, and walked along carrying him piggy-backed style while he talked softly with him as the men rode on ahead into the village.

"Grandfather," the boy asked finally, "can I go with you? I do not want to stay here by myself like this."

"Oh? Do you have some problem you want to talk about?"

"Well, I just don't belong here, that's all."

"You cannot go back to the Pod, you know that, don't you?"

"No, not to live there, like before. But I can go with you. I can go anywhere you go, and live anywhere you live." He had obviously thought it through.

As they came into the village Babineau let him down to walk alongside under his own steam. They climbed the front steps of the town hall together, passing old Juanita sitting there on her chair in the afternoon sun, waiting for them. As they passed she looked up at Henri in askance, but he simply leaned over and asked her quietly to have Rosa send the boy's things across; he would be joining the single men in their quarters.

As they entered the building Sola took his hand again, looking up at him said, "I don't want to live with those boys in the dormitory, Grandfather, I want to stay with you."

Babineau nodded, and took him through to his apartment where, grubby and weary after the long day, he stripped off his dirty working clothes and tossing a towel over his shoulder headed off to the ablution block. Halfway down the corridor he turned, chuckling at the way Sola had copied him exactly, like he was a grown man, and was following him into the shower where a few of the other, younger unmarried men were already attending to their ablutions.

"How old are you now, boy?" he asked.

"Nearly twelve."

"Can you ride?"

"Of course, better than some."

Babineau looked down at him, smiling. "I bet you can."

"OK," he continued, "you want to work for me, eh? You want to be a gaucho, and run cattle, eh?"

Sola left his towel on the wooden railing, then stepped over to one of the shower heads beside the other men and set the warm water over his body, taking some soap and a cloth to wash himself up and down before looking back up at Babineau, considering the question and taking his time to answer. By then the old man had his own shower going, and rather than rush him simply set about soaping himself.

Before long Sola had finished, and turning off the water he stepped across and took his towel to dry himself. When he was done he wrapped it around himself then sat on the bench waiting for Babineau to finish. This time he copied the boy, and as he finished drying himself he wrapped the towel around his middle then sat patiently, waiting for the boy to speak.

"Grandfather," he started finally, "I want to help the poor starving people in the famine areas. You can teach me, then I can go and help them."

Babineau sat quietly before glancing down at the boy still staring earnestly up at him. His resigned sigh caused the boy to redden deeply, embarrassed, and cry angrily in protest.

"It's true! I know, I saw the film footage. It was all over the news, on every station!"

"OK, OK, OK," the old man replied gently, then stood and went to go. After a few paces he turned to wait for him, and Sola got up from the bench to follow, while two of the men watched them go, smiling and shaking their heads.

As they made their way back down the corridor Babineau paused once more, and turning to the boy said, "Well, my young friend, we had better go and have a look then, eh?"

While they dressed Sola kept looking at the old man, until finally he said, "You have to get a TV for the hall, as well."

Babineau looked at him, astonished. "We have no electricity," he replied simply.

"I can run some cables across from the gate. We can pick up the signal there too." He looked up again, determined now, and went on. "You can't be so ignorant of what is happening out there in the big wide world. The grownups can watch the news, and learn about what is happening, and the kids can watch movies."

"You have to come up to date eventually," he finished, pleading.

The old man sat, shaking his head. "Holy Mother, what have I done," he muttered to himself.

He stared at the boy for a moment, then started to say, "But this is the big world out here," then thought better of it.

"Well at least you will know what they are broadcasting finally," Sola added, interrupting him, defensive now.

"That's true." Babineau stood to go. "We shall see about it then, eh? Let's go look at the world first, then we shall see about it."

At the door he stopped, and turned. "I might as well tell you I am to retire anyway. Emilio will be the new boss. The men know, but we will let the families know at dinner tonight." He then disappeared through the corridor into the main hall while Sola hurried after him.

Neatly piled on the table were his clothes, with his toys and gadgets piled into cartons on the floor. He glanced through them, annoyed that Rosa did not know a radio antenna from a length of fencing wire, which of course to everyone else looked exactly alike despite the cabling soldered neatly to one end, and had jumbled everything together; to rid her house of it all, he suspected.

Babineau sat in the next chair to him, inspecting the cartons and watching his expression.

"You must be very clever to have made all of this, just out of bits lying around," he said gently.

"But it is all ruined. I won't be able to reconnect everything in time, before we go."

"Oh, throw it away. On the way back we can stop of and buy you some new gear. Proper gear, OK? How does that sound?"

"Really?" his eyes lit up, then narrowed a little, cautious now. "You promise!"

"I promise," the other said, holding his gaze. "I have never lied to you, son."

He then took his face in his hands, holding him close while he continued to talk softly to him, persuading him. "Take it outside, and the boys will use some of it. The rest can go to the tip."

Sola hesitated, then one by one picked up the cartons and left them outside on the porch. Without a word he then took up his clothes and went through the corridor to grandpa's rooms, and sat folding them neatly into the trunk next to his bed.

When he finished, he stripped again of his dirty clothes and changed into a clean shirt and trousers, then went down to the bathroom where he wet and combed his hair neatly before going back out into the hall where some of the men were starting to gather.

As he drew near the old man reached over and tousled his hair, messing it again into cute spikes, then smiling at him contentedly said, "No more talk now. Tonight we have a big party, and you can keep my beer topped up for me, OK?"

The boy nodded, then went over and poured him a large glass of cold beer from the keg they had brought up from the cellar, which he sipped appreciatively. As he sat down and handed it across one of the other men placed a small beer in front of him as well, then winked as they all raised their glasses.

After that first beer he did not want any more, but continued to get up and fill Babineau's glass as it was slowly emptied. One of the women finally brought him a glass of tea, admonishing the men for giving him beer, with which to wash down his meal.

Even then it was early when he nodded off, and leaned snoring against his grandfather until he picked him up and carried him to bed. As he tucked him in, he leaned over and brushed his snowy blond hair aside and kissed him lightly on the forehead, then sat back studying his face awhile before heading thoughtfully back to the party out in the main hall.

Despite the festivity next morning they were up early, and ate their breakfast quietly in the soft grey pre-dawn light. The others joining them were Raol, whose family were from one of the outer villages away from the gate, and Luisito who was only a little older than Sola. He was called Luisito to distinguish him from his father Luis, Emilio the new boss's younger brother.

By the time they had finished their coffee they heard the soft thud of hooves and gentle nickering of horses outside, so they tidied up and went out onto the porch. At the top of the steps Babineau stopped and turned.

"Sola, where did you say the people were starving?" he wanted to know.

"There is a refugee camp outside of Bazada, in Nirrim."

One of the men looked up, and he nodded. The man turned his horse and rode off toward the gate while they stepped down off the porch and took their reins. Sola was allowed to ride his favourite stock horse, that he loved to ride because it was so quick and smart, and knew what he wanted just from the shift of his body. He checked his gear thoroughly, but when he went to take up the girth the animal sucked in a deep breath and stood, ribs out, trying to make him leave the strap a little loose. The boy was having none of that, and frustrated, punched it sharply behind the rib cage then as she let go quickly pulled the strap tight and buckled it.

His grandfather was watching him, and smiled, causing his face to flush red in embarrassment.

"She will be good!" he protested. "She is just sleepy, and doesn't want to go yet."

"That's OK, son. You did well. Don't worry about it."

Then all mounted the four of them set off toward the gate. As they rode Babineau explained to them the warp technique they would use on this trip, bypassing the usual relay deep beneath the Pod and going instead directly to their destination.

"We do not usually go this way if we have new travelers with us. The slightly longer delay may make you nauseous, and we do not know enough about other effects," he was saying. "When we get through, if you feel odd in any way put up your hand, like this."

Sola put up his hand as shown.

"Luisito, you too," Raol said. "You are not so clever."

So both boys obediently raised their hands, and as they drew nearer the gate listened intently now to the instructions they were being given. Riding up onto the gate itself they were waved straight through without losing stride, ears attuned in the dim grey twilight of in-between to the steady creaking of leather and rhythmic sway of the horses in order to maintain their rhythm and their sense of time passing, keeping themselves synchronised. Quickly they came out again into bright sunlight, the air dry and hot with a gusting wind whipping up small dust devils around them.

As soon as they were all clear they stopped and looked around. Babineau caught their eye each in turn, and they all shrugged, and nodded everything OK, so he pulled his kerchief up around his nose and mouth against the dust, and rode on ahead. The other three did likewise and followed abreast.

Looking around, Sola could see that the area around this gate was subject to sand storms, set up on a rock shelf above what appeared to be an extensive dune system they had to traverse in order to reach what looked like a large village or town away in the distance, much larger it seemed than their own home village.

"What place is that?" he called to Babineau, but Raol instead leaned over and told him it was Bazada. He then tapped his arm, and catching his line of sight pointed away to the east, away from the town toward a great grey smudge on the horizon.

"Bazada Fair," he said. "We go there, not Bazada."

"Is that the refugee camp, where the people are dying?" Sola wanted to know.

Raol looked at him sharply, shaking his head. "No refugee! Big market, big trading port, you see for yourself, OK?"

With that the older man rode on ahead to be with Babineau, leaving the two boys to follow on behind. For the rest of the day they made steady progress across the dune beds, until late in the afternoon as the trail topped a small rise they could see a vast shimmering lake stretched out before them, then turning north along the shore made their way into the outskirts of the great sprawling fairground.

Babineau began to draw ahead a little, as Raol dropped back to ride with the boys.

"The Fair is all eyes and ears," he cautioned them. "Say nothing, and do nothing to draw attention to yourself. Let your grandfather do the talking, OK?"

They both nodded and he took up a station a neck ahead of them to form a precise order of riding with Babineau maintaining his position a full length in front. As they rode men called out in greeting, which the old man returned in elaborate ceremony and long-winded repartee.

The boys watched keenly as they made their way through the deepening crowd milling about in the evening dusk, then quite suddenly they turned aside into a compound just off the main thoroughfare where Sola was surprised to see Luisito's older brother Samuel emerge from a doorway to take their horses in hand.

Confused now, and tired after the long ride, he simply nodded in acquiescence and dismounted as he was bidden. Babineau turned to watch him, and when he stood there not moving as the horses were led away, leaving him standing there alone, he went over to turn his hat back, and lift his grimy face now streaked with tears and weariness.

He looked up, then down again, shaking his head, his lip quivering. The old man knelt before him, taking his face in his hands kindly, but not saying anything just watching him. He broke sharply away, embarrassed, before turning back again.

"It's all stupid!" he cried. "I can't bloody do anything right."

"Hey, hey, it's not your fault." Babineau took him by the shoulders and held him firmly, looking directly into his eyes. "Son, it is not your fault."

He melted then, and flung himself sobbing into his arms. In the one movement he was picked up and carried inside, but he fought and found himself let down again onto his own two feet.

"OK," Babineau replied, "come and get cleaned up, and we will have something to eat. It has been a very long day."

Trusting him that much Sola still angry and confused followed him as he entered the main building, then passing through came out onto a row of huts. There was a duck-walk running along the front, and he could see there was a central ablution block and over to the left a larger hut toward which he found himself being steered. Inside there was a woven carpet with a stove in the middle. The style of it pulled him up, not the layout as such. It reminded him of Babineau's apartment up in the Pod, and as he looked about him and thought about it not unlike his own place back home.

The familiarity of it brought him back to his senses, and as he looked up the other nodded. They went about their business, and taking their towels went out along the duck-walk to the showers where without a lot of soap, and not too much water, they managed to get the grime off and feel at least partly human once more.

The simple resonance of being there again was good, and as they followed their usual habit, and dressed, and followed each other out into the dining hut where their meal was ready on the table waiting for them. They all relaxed and sat quietly awhile, attending to the food on their plate.

Eventually Sola said, without looking up, "Grandfather, where is the Holy City?"

"Where did you hear that, son?" the old man asked.

"It was being called out to you in the street, out there. 'How are they in the Holy City,' they said, and you cried back, 'Hola, God is merciful.' I just didn't know where it was is all."

"How did you know the language?" Raol asked from offside.

Sola glanced up, and down again, then slowly up, embarrassed again. "I taught myself Nirrimese, through the implant in my head, when I thought I was going to come out here to do refugee work," he explained.

Babineau leaned over, watching him intently now. "How did you log in? I thought the Pod had you classified as processed, and deleted your file."

"Oh, that was when I was little, when I was eight, before I came out with you. But then I figured out how to hack through the firewall and set up my own system permissions, so I created a new file of my own. I am the *Night Rider*," he declared, "I can do what I want in there and they can't catch me."

"They originally thought I was a virus," he went on, "but they couldn't find me and I wasn't causing any harm, so after a while they just gave up. Now I can skip in and out and do what I want, so long as I do not interrupt any of the TSR programs running in memory."

The old man sat shaking his head. "We know nothing of these things," he muttered.

"I tried to explain, honest, but Auntie Rosa kept hitting me, and sending me out to chop firewood." Sola protested, but the other held up his hand to silence him.

"We know nothing of these things, son. And you will say no more of it, to anyone, ever. Do you understand?"

He nodded.

"Luisito, Samuel, do you understand?"

They were both trembling slightly, their eyes glazed over with superstitious dread, but they nodded and the room went silent.

After a moment Raol broke in. "Young nephew," he said, "You say you can speak Nirrimese. Is that so?"

"Yes, I can speak fluently. I can learn any language. The teaching algorithms are excellent."

"OK, OK, OK," Babineau stopped him there.

"I am sorry, grandfather," the boy said. "I try to do well. I try to be good. Honest. But I can't help it if people don't understand what I am saying." He sat there slumped, miserable and confused again, as tears ran down his cheeks once more.

"It's OK. Don't cry. Nobody is angry with you. At least we know now where all this is headed." He glanced across at Raol, and nodded, then went on, "We can use a good translator. Do you want the job?"

Sola looked up, confused. "I thought you were going to punish me."

"No. No, son. It's OK. Everything is all right." He paused for a moment. "You are a young man now. You are with us. Your business is your own business, but we will support you until you find your feet. If you need to return to your studies, we will cover that. Anything you need is OK. Just tell us if you want the job."

He looked across at Raol, then back to his grandfather. "Of course I want the job. Of course, it's perfect!"

"It's done, then." Babineau smacked his hand gently on the table, then turned calling Samuel to bring some beer so they could drink on it.

As they waited Sola leaned forward, and asked, "Grandfather, you haven't told me yet where is the Holy City."

The old man turned, gazing at him directly, unflinching. "The Holy City is the Pod. We work for the Pod. That is what this is all about. The Holy City is you, young Sola, and in you we now have a piece of it."

Book III

Sola's head hurt. He was taking more and more time away from the gate system, no longer warping through even with his own gauchos as it left him nauseated, dizzy, disoriented. Instead he'd lie down in the men's quarters and take a nap, dreaming his own dreams, playing his own mind games so as to keep his implant volume as low as possible, and shut out the constant intrusion.

Refreshed more or less, he'd wander down through the village to the sun-baked plaza, to find Henri with the old men playing cards under the great shady banyan trees where they transacted all their business.

They wouldn't allow him to play, he knew, because he won all the time. His mind simply ran too fast, recalculating the odds as he followed the cards exactly as they fell, while his stake grew and grew and grew, until they stood one after the other yelling at him to leave them in peace.

If he did that he was allowed to sit and watch occasionally, except since his headaches started Henri made space for him at his own table; murmuring quietly to him as he played, crooning almost.

They were at cards like that when the news came, the gaggle of dark, swarthy old men and the one small blond boy with the tiny row of lights flickering through the pale skin at the back of his head. The day was fine and warm; the reek of rough tobacco and strong coffee aroma hanging over them in the still air the way they liked it, in no small part because it kept the women at a distance.

Sola was dozing almost, breathing steadily with his head down not thinking much, until suddenly he jerked upright. The old men looked up from their cards; not at him but up the road at his Auntie Rosa running toward them, screaming and crying.

He didn't have a chance until later to say anything; they'd all supposed that like them he was simply looking up at Rosa.

When his turn to speak did come finally he decided it didn't matter much what they thought, so he only told Henri, Raol and Luisito that somebody had done something to short-circuit the gate.

He was feeling a lot better since his headache had gone now, except that he had a bad gut-feeling and wanted to know what on earth was going on.

Rosa overheard the exchange and started yelling at him not to be so stupid; who in Christ's Holy Fucking Name did he think he was, but his grandmother Juanita told her to be quiet, watching him closely for anything he might be thinking.

"Bring the boy, Henri," she called across.

Henri led the way into the village hall and through the big common room down the long corridor to Juanita's infirmary and quarters.

The head gaucho Emilio was laid out delirious on clean linen sheets, alternately sweating and shivering. His glands were swollen and weeping and the lymph nodes under his lower jaw, and in his arm pits and groin, formed great dark festering lumps.

Juanita had taken the precaution of burning Emilio's clothes and had the room strewn with sage and wormwood. After gazing about the room Sola studied her thoughtfully. There never seemed to be much to say between them, as if they mutually considered speaking to one another superfluous, so once he'd absorbed what he needed to know he simply turned on his heel and made his way up the track to where the gate stood.

As he approached the gate shimmered and hummed suddenly and more of the men came through; their leader Luis limping badly and two of his crew carrying another on a makeshift stretcher.

He ran straight past, ignoring them to swiftly locate residual signal before the gate shimmer faded, and with it any time/space coordinates lingering from their passage.

He stopped abruptly, stunned, then turned on his heel and ran quickly back to the village hall.

"What's up?" Henri reached out to hold him, asking quietly.

"What are they doing in Medieval Europe, grandfather, I mean, fourteenth century? They are not supposed to go there. They have the plague, and been caught up in some sort of war. Please, get everyone outside. Don't let them come in. Don't let anyone go near them."

He ran back up the track, stopping the men from entering the village. He made them strip off their clothes and pile them in a heap which he fired.

The man on the stretcher was badly hurt with stab wounds and Luis had a long bleeding gash down his thigh, but Sola refused to allow them to move. Instead he ran back again to bring a big jar of Juanita's poultice, and more herbs and clean water that he made Rosa carry for him.

He had them bathe where they stood, especially their hair and armpits, and their groins and underparts, telling them to check thoroughly to ensure they were carrying no insects or anything else that might leap from person to person. Then he made them rub the poultice well in, all over their bodies.

Only then did he let them pass, before stripping himself naked and piling his own clothes on the roaring fire; washing himself thoroughly the same way.

Back at the long house he wrapped a new cloth about his loins and took Henri and Raol aside, leaving the rest to Juanita and Auntie Rosa while he spoke. Quickly they nodded and turned to follow the others, demanding a thorough debriefing while he went back up to the gate.

Signing in through his *Night Rider* account he promptly logged into the Pod's computers.

His confidence had grown since the gauchos gave him the job of translating and interpreting for them, and once they could see their advantage encouraging him to stay sitting out there at the gate accessing the Pod system; excusing him from the work of the village.

He'd remained a loner, with his clipped, formal, semi-cyborg speech accented only by the rough village dialect. Rosa still beat him, regarding him as autistic, but not so badly now. Henri loved him with a passion without knowing why, and protected him as he could, while his old crone grandmother Juanita considered him touched, blessed, a seer, and he was still only fourteen.

Little did they know, any of them.

Focussing all his attention on the digital media transponder implanted at the back of his skull, there from birth, he set up a search algorithm. As it ran he sat back with his eyes closed watching the code scroll past, line after line after line.

Eventually words began to stand out, not clear code but AKAs, aliases such as hackers use . . . . *Th3D3f3nd3r*, *warpgoddess*, *kali666ma*. He went back to check his own name *Night Rider*.

His jaw dropped. Whoever they were they were using his port, a gaming port he'd thought was derelict. Podlings are banned from playing computer games. All the gaming ports in the Pod system had been locked centuries ago, until that night he'd opened one himself thinking nobody would notice. That's how he'd been able to sign himself in and out.

But somebody had noticed. Somebody was using the port to play games.

He abruptly logged off. They may have noticed him but they may not. Muttering to himself, deeply troubled, he wandered slowly back down through the village, avoiding people as he went.

Rosa and Henri watched him from across the street.

"What did you discover, lad?"

"There are podling kids in there mucking around," he called back. "They got in through my gaming port. They think it is all one big war game. That is why I was getting my headaches, now I know, with them mucking around in there. It stopped when Emilio used the emergency override on that old medieval gate in Avignon to return home, when he found people were dying."

He paused a moment before continuing. "That old gate, you know; in Avignon, you must remember it grandfather. It has been locked since Pope Clement went to live there, when they were warring over whether popes or kings should rule the world. It became too dangerous for us to come and go like we do, do you remember, so the gate was locked."

"OK, yes, I know, but the other men didn't come through there. They found themselves in Scotland, so they tell me."

"Yes. Falkirk. They came back through Falkirk. Did Emilio say anything to you about that? He must have done something to get them away from there. That gate had not been used either, but a lot earlier, since the Normans."

"Emilio died, son. He didn't get a chance to say anything."

Sola looked away but quickly shook the thought out of his mind. They'll have to move fast. "All right," he said instead, "I will do it. I will run some tests."

But the gathered village was staring coldly at him by this time. Some were crossing themselves, and muttering oaths. Henri went over and instead of allowing him to leave, took him in hand and led him up the steps into the long house, closing the big front door behind them.

"Tell me simply, Sola, what do you think has happened?"

He sat back, waiting, as the boy pondered the question, brow puckered and sucking his lower lip.

"Well," he said finally, "if you remember, when you picked me up, that first time we met, what had happened was I learned to turned the volume down; of this thing inside my head."

"It was boring. I sort of, came out of it, and became myself instead. I had my own thoughts after that, you must remember, and kept forgetting about it, and got logged out. Grandfather, you do remember."

Henri nodded, glancing away and back again.

"There are more loose kids in there," Sola continued, "inside the Pod; podling kids. I think they went the other way from me. What I mean is, they went into the implant itself, a bit like I did later, once I realised I could. But they have never been out anywhere, not outside, to find themselves, as persons, like, so they do not realise there is an outside world out here as well as their own inside world."

He paused, shaking his head slowly. "They think the implant system is real. They think the wars are real. They think the Pod is actually fighting all these wars against evil. You know," he paused, frustrated, "we already talked about all that."

Henri stood thoughtfully and went over to the big stove for hot water, and coming back made them both coffee.

"So, how do we get through to them?" he asked finally, as he placed a hot cup before Sola then sat back and blew on his own to cool it.

"Well, we cannot. Not really, they are oblivious. They have sort of, become part of the Pod I guess, you know; wired into the system. Their bodies and nervous systems have most likely merged with the electronics by now. It would not have taken very long."

Henri gazed thoughtfully at him, nodding gently, but then he cocked his head a moment, curious.

"What, grandfather?"

"You can see them, son, can't you?"

"Ah, well, not really. I have to explain, but you don't know how the computers work, except, like, when I log in I am aware of them, because they leave traces in all the system registries, like I do if I don't erase them, and clean up before I log out."

"The system will create files and registry entries for every user who logs into their account. It is automatic."

"Do you mean like a human or an animal leaves footprints?"

Sola pricked up, eyes bright, "Yes, like that. If I left such traces behind like they do the system would be able to track me, and the antivirus program would find me and delete me."

He stopped a moment, thinking. "Anyway, that's how I can see where they have been, and where they are likely to be; it is so easy, they are not viruses like me, nor trojans; they are end-users, properly certified. They will never be deleted."

Henri nodded again. "But if they do know about this *Night Rider* character they know about me too; would I be correct?"

"Well, yes, sometimes I leave a little avatar of me, as the *Night Rider*. It is like a little picture of me, but with hell tattoos like yours, grandfather. Sometimes I leave it in one of their user directories, like a calling card. It is for fun."

The old man stood once more, and going across to his bureau in the corner took some paper and a pencil. Setting the boy's cup aside he placed them before him.

"All right, draw me a picture of this *Night Rider*."

"Must I do so?" Sola hesitated. "I have an image already in the system. All I have to do is display it once I have logged in, and everybody can see."

"But we can't, can we? There's no way we can see."

"Go on, lad; show me what you look like when you go in there."

The boy blushed scarlet. "You will not be angry at me?"

"Depends, doesn't it? I'll a lot madder if you don't; you can bank all your card winnings on that."

Sola stared at him a moment before picking up the pencil. He paused and said, "It would be better if you get me some colour pencils."

Henri stood and did so, then sat waiting while Sola did as he was bid.

When he finished he sat back grinning sheepishly.

The old man reached over and flicked the page around, pulling it toward him. He raised his eyebrows and nodded.

"So, what's all this about. Making fun of me, is it?"

"No! I am not making fun of you. I thought it was inspired. I am your translator, is that right? That main head tattoo is from you, grandfather, but those two side tattoos are ancient writing symbols; icons. They are wings, from Hermes, the messenger. They are called talaria."

Henri's jaw dropped, and his face broke into a broad smile. He chuckled and reached over and tousled the boy's fine white hair.

"What would happen, do you think, if we both arrived like that inside the Pod, together, and got into where these kids are?"

"Hell," Sola grinned, "they would shit themselves."

The other looked at him, and then nodded. "All right, we'll do it."

He stood and went to the door, beckoning Rosa inside before calling one of the boys to go fetch Raol. Rosa followed him to the infirmary where he called in on Juanita, sitting there at her desk reading; her patients bandaged and asleep. He bade her come.

Back at the big dining table he showed them Sola's drawing, explaining that the two of them had to enter the Pod together in an official capacity. He wanted them as senior village elders to approve Sola's tattoos, his new facial tattoos signifying his status as their properly certified translator.

Rosa opened her mouth wide, starting to yell angrily at them, but he glared her down until Raol quietly nodded first, then Juanita.

There was silence, then, "Yes, I agree," Rosa said finally. "Maybe if he looks less like an idiot, he'll behave less like an idiot. That will be a blessing."

Henri glanced at Raol who went across to his room in the old men's quarters and brought back his tattooing needles and jars of brightly coloured ink. At that they sat the boy down and shaved his head.

Juanita had an astringent lotion which also acted as local anaesthetic, which Henri thought might be a good idea if they were to do the whole job at once. He asked Sola quietly if he was ready, and the boy nodded and leaned forward.

When his pate was done Raol lifted his chin. His eyes were clear and steady, merely glistening, so when Henri leaned in to suggest cheek stripes either side; not three as he had but one on either cheek, he agreed. Single cheek stripes denoted, they all knew, that while this slim fourteen year-old who looked but ten was not to be considered of rank, he was highly respected nonetheless.

When they were finished they stood him up, and he wobbled slightly on his feet before quickly gaining his composure. He declined a mirror, simply holding his head awhile under a cold tap at the sink before drying himself off with the cloth from around his waist, then indicated they'd better leave.

It would not take very long before Emilio's gate over-rides had been repaired; probably automatically at midnight as each of the computers in turn defragmented and reboot, but they had no way of knowing whether somebody might already be on the job.

Because they were merely entering the Pod, not running cattle or driving transports, Henri and Sola made their way up the wide track to the gate clad only in robes. The entire village, awe-struck, lined the way.

Once through the gate shimmer Henri induced, as was his rank prerogative, they made their way immediately to the change rooms and disrobed, then into the disinfectant showers and up through the air locks before taking the elevator directly to his private apartment.

His valet Philippe attended them on arrival, his buzzer having at once alerted him to his master's presence within the warp gate.

Despite the housekeeper's stone face, astonishment at the sight of the boy with his shining skull marked by vivid fresh tattooing registered only a flicker of eyebrow. His polished subservience quickly killed any hint of what might be going on in his mind.

"We have a crisis, Monsieur," he said simply. "The Ministry is assembled, and awaiting your arrival."

"We have an important errand to run, Philippe, a message to deliver. You may inform the Ministry of my presence within the city, and that I will attend them the moment my task is done. Go now, immediately. On return you will accompany us, as witness, but right now you are to say nothing of this to the Assembly."

As they waited for Philippe to return they donned their Pod clothing; Sola in his old lime green satin briefs under coveralls and Henri in his Kadian uniform.

On reflection, Henri had Sola change back into Luisito's old childhood uniform and at least look official.

That was the first time the boy had a chance to see himself in a mirror and he ducked away in alarm.

"Ah, conditioned reflex," Henri said. "You haven't quite got over it yet, have you? Come here, son."

He held him steady at the mirror while the boy absorbed the new image of himself; not the make-believe play-thing he'd been imagining as he hacked the vast complex of computers, but by mimesis and natural age transition what he'd become.

He turned his body slowly this way and that, watching himself, back and front.

Finally he nodded and Henri let him go, to wander about the apartment, inspecting the shields and armaments of Kadian rank and privilege, until Philippe knocked softly and they turned to leave.

Outside on the street Sola stopped, confused for a moment. He closed his eyes, turning on his heel scanning ahead, then took a handkerchief from his pocket and made a blindfold to cover his eyes. Sightless he made his way unerringly along the narrow streets, turning and turning back again as the tiny lights of his implant flickered rapidly, to find a new elevator taking them to yet another level.

"This is a restricted zone, Monsieur," Philippe said finally, which only goaded Sola. The manservant reluctantly followed.

They came to a shop selling outer-world decorative craftwork and went inside. Making their way through shelving to the rear Sola began feeling with his fingers along the mock timber wall panelling.

He stopped, satisfied, and removing his blindfold stood there immobile. In his mind he logged into the system. A moment later as he finished decrypting the security they heard a soft click. He felt along a rail above his head until he found a lever, and as he pulled it a low door swung open.

The two men ducked their heads to enter.

The place hummed.

And it stank.

The floor was piled high with empty pizza cartons, hamburger wrappers and milkshake containers. Heavy metal blasted from huge speakers.

In the middle of the room, before an array of consoles, sat a row of what looked like fat podlings, except these were clad in skin-tight body suits with wires everywhere connected back into their consoles.

Henri watched astonished as a video orgy played on one of the screens and the body sequestered before it spasmed suddenly in climax. A fat hand reached down to wipe itself with a tissue that was tossed carelessly among the detritus.

Sola turned and nodded, then closed his eyes. A moment later each console screen flickered into synch; changing to display a huge picture of Henri and himself, with him standing forward to take up the foreground; their intricate tattoos of rank vibrant with colour.

The speakers went silent until slowly, almost in a dream state, each set of pudgy eyes turned to see their super heroes standing there in the flesh.

"FUCK!"

Philippe turned and left. A few minutes later he returned with a squad of armed security who promptly rang for technicians.

Henri and Sola were ushered quickly out, not back through the secret door but into an elevator where they sped down into the core of the Pod with its labyrinthine ministerial chambers.

The assembly sat silently. The crisis appeared over. Henri merely stepped forward and approached the speaker of the house before turning back to ensure Sola was safe. With him there at his side he bowed solemnly, then formally presented the boy as his designated translator and ambassador.

On their way out again hundreds of eyes followed, but as they left the chamber a great clamour erupted.

Back in the elevator Sola asked, finally, "Do you think we will get into trouble?"

"Nah! Trouble is, you know, they're all stupid."

The boy nodded solemnly.

"Maybe we should not go off fighting any more of their wars, do you think? If I stay awhile, and log in any time I want, maybe we can get them all to believe something else."

"Like what?"

"I think, like, maybe, there is no such thing as evil. What would that be like? There would be nothing to be fighting over or worrying about, just sort of, peaceful, and happy."

"Not sure if I agree with that, son. We'd all be out of a job, wouldn't we? We wouldn't be their bloody heroes, would we, just ordinary farmers."

"But we are ordinary farmers. There is nothing else."

Henri gazed down at him.

"Why don't we go to my club for dinner? We can join a game of bridge, or backgammon if you really want to win money. These old guys won't yell at you; you'll be a legend."

"Really? Do you think so?"

"I know so."

THE END

PodWarp

ABOUT THE AUTHOR

As an anthropologist, novelist and writer Gil Hardwick is a gifted author. Over many years working as a field ethnographer in the vast Australian inland he has met real characters and had real-life adventures, bringing his personalities and his plots to vibrant life. Writing from life, he neither shies away from real social issues and at times confronting dilemmas.

Well worth reading.

PodWarp